GREENWICH LIBRARIES	
WE	
3 8028 02102030 7	
Askews & Holts	16-Aug-2013
JF D .	£4.99
3997297	

First published 2009 by Macmillan Children's Books
This edition published 2013 by Macmillan Children's Books
a division of Macmillan Publishers Limited
20 New Wharf Road, London N1 9RR
Basingstoke and Oxford
Associated companies throughout the world
www.panmacmillan.com

ISBN: 978-1-4472-3528-6

Text copyright © Julia Donaldson 2009
Illustrations copyright © Lydia Monks 2009
Moral rights asserted

All rights reserved. No part of this publication may be reproduced, stored in or
introduced into a retrieval system, or transmitted in any form, or by any means,
(electronic, mechanical, photocopying, recording or otherwise) without the prior
written permission of the publisher. Any person who does any unauthorized
act in relation to this publication may be liable to criminal prosecution
and civil claims for damages.

2 4 6 8 9 7 5 3 1

A CIP catalogue record for this book is available from the British Library.

Printed in China

What the
Ladybird Heard

Julia Donaldson

Illustrated by Lydia Monks

MACMILLAN CHILDREN'S BOOKS

Once upon a farm lived a fat red hen,
A duck in a pond and a goose in a pen,
A woolly sheep, a hairy hog,
A handsome horse and a dainty dog,

A cat that miaowed and a cat that purred,
A fine prize cow . . . and a ladybird.

And the cow said, "MOO!"

and the hen said, "CLUCK!"

"HISS!" said the goose

and "QUACK!" said the duck.

"NEIGH!"
said the horse.

"OINK!" said the hog.

"BAA!" said the sheep

and "WOOF!"
said the dog.

One cat miaowed while
the other one purred . . .

9

And the ladybird said never a word.

But the ladybird saw,
And the ladybird heard . . .

She saw two men in a big black van,
With a map and a key and a cunning plan.
And she heard them whisper, "This is how
We're going to steal the fine prize cow:

"Open the gate at dead of night.
Pass the horse and then turn right.
Round the duck pond, past the hog
(Be careful not to wake the dog).

Left past the sheep, then straight ahead
And in through the door of the prize cow's shed!"

And the little spotty ladybird
(Who never before had said a word)
Told the animals, "This is how
Two thieves are planning to steal the cow:
They'll open the gate at dead of night.
Pass the horse and then turn right.

Round the duck pond, past the hog
(Being careful not to wake the dog).
Left past the sheep, then straight ahead
And in through the door of the prize cow's shed!"

And the cow said, "MOO!"

and the hen said,
"CLUCK!"

"HISS!" said the goose

and "QUACK!"
said the duck.

"NEIGH!" said the horse.

"OINK!" said the hog.

"BAA!" said the sheep.

"WOOF!" said the dog.

And both the cats began to miaow:
"We can't let them steal the fine prize cow!"

But the ladybird had a good idea

And she whispered it into each animal ear.

At dead of night the two bad men
(Hefty Hugh and Lanky Len)
Opened the gate while the farmer slept
And tiptoe into the farm they crept.

Then the goose said, "NEIGH!" with all her might.
And Len said, "That's the horse — turn right."

And the dainty dog began to QUACK.
"The duck!" said Hugh.
"We're right on track."

"OINK," said the cats.
"There goes the hog!
Be careful not to wake the dog."

"BAA BAA BAA," said the fat red hen.
"The sheep! We're nearly there," said Len.

Then the duck on the pond said, "MOO MOO MOO!"
"Two more steps to go!" said Hugh.

MOO!

And they both stepped into the duck pond —
SPLOSH!

And the farmer woke and said, "Golly gosh!"
And he called the cops, and they came — NEE NAH!
And they threw the thieves in their panda car.

Then the cow said, "MOO!"

and the hen said,
"CLUCK!"

"HISS!" said the goose

and "QUACK!"
said the duck.

"NEIGH!" said the horse.

"OINK!"
said the hog.

"BAA!" said the sheep.

"WOOF!"
said the dog.

And the farmer cheered, and both cats purred.

But the ladybird said never a word.

What the Ladybird Heard

About the author and illustrator

Julia Donaldson has written some of the world's favourite
picture books. She also writes books for older children, as well as
plays and songs. Unlike the quiet little ladybird, Julia likes to spend
a lot of time on stage performing her brilliant sing-along shows!

Lydia Monks is an award-winning illustrator with many picture
books to her name. She has illustrated characters as varied
in size as a mermaid, a spider, a rabbit and a bear.
But none of them are as tiny as the ladybird.

D0320579